APRIL FOOLS' DAY
FROM THE
BLACK LAGOON

APRIL FOOLS' DAY
FROM THE
BLACK LAGOON

by Mike Thaler
Illustrated by Jared Lee

SCHOLASTIC INC.

New York Toronto London Auckland Sydney
Mexico City New Delhi Hong Kong Buenos Aires

To Dave, Ali, & Family
—M.T.

To Dave Clevenger, Class Clown
—J.L.

ISBN-13: 978-0-545-01767-1
ISBN-10: 0-545-01767-X

Text copyright © 2008 by Mike Thaler
Illustrations copyright © 2008 by Jared D. Lee Studio, Inc.

12 11 10 9 8 7 6   9 10 11 12 13/0

Printed in the U.S.A.
First printing, April 2008

CONTENTS

MARCHING

CHAPTER 1
PRANKSGIVING

I always get excited toward the end of March as we march toward April. I both look forward to and dread April 1st . . . April Fools' Day.*

* SEE PAGE 63

BAD IDEA PRANK #1

7

I look forward to the pranks I will play on innocent, unsuspecting victims . . . but dread the pranks that will be played on me.

REMEMBER THE TIME I PUT DOG FOOD IN YOUR SANDWICH?

THAT WAS A GOOD ONE.

There are always the good old standbys—the whoopee cushion, the rubber tarantula, plastic vomit, and the fly in the ice cube. But I stretch for the unusual, the extraordinary, the embarrassing.

I've already come up with some good ones—substituting hot sauce in the ketchup container, switching the signs on the girls' and boys' bathrooms, and hiding all the toilet paper.

These are only preliminary ideas and need to be refined. The only thing I know for sure that I'm going to do is put Mom's pantyhose in the freezer.

FREEZER →

PANTYHOSE

CHAPTER 2
THE THINK PRANK

On the bus everyone is quiet and thinking. They're all deep in thought working on their pranks. Every so often someone will snicker and look over at me. Uh-oh, they've got a good one!

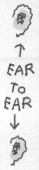

If I ask, "What's so funny?" they say, "Oh, nothing," then they smile and look out the window grinning from ear to ear. This is going to be horrible, a real April Ghouls' Day.

EAR
TO
EAR

FRESH MEAT
↓

SNICKER. SNICKER.

TEE HEE HEE.

HA HA.

SCHOOL BUS

NO 13

13

I need to form a league of nations, an alliance uniting the boys, so all the pranks will be played on the girls. Then I think, *That wouldn't be fair. But on the other hand . . . it would work.*

CHAPTER 3
A TIGER IN YOUR PRANK

However, at recess none of the guys want to limit their creativity in any way. Even Eric, my best buddy, smiles and says, "Just wait and see." This is bad. I may not even come to school on April 1st.

In class, Mrs. Green cautions us to keep our pranks in good taste and harmless fun. Then Eric smiles like a mad scientist and says, "Just wait and see." I

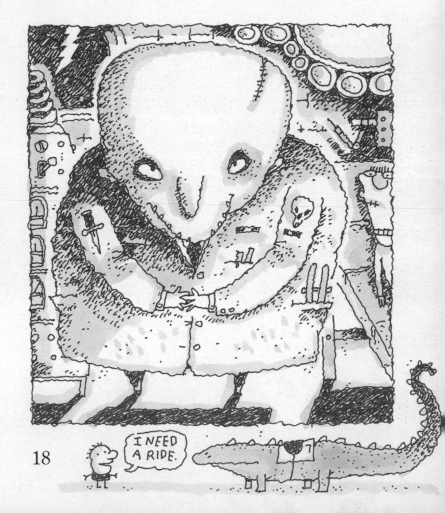

I NEED A RIDE.

raise my hand and suggest we
skip April Fools' Day altogether
and make it a day of peace and
brotherhood. The girls and I are
the only ones who vote for it.

Then I suggest that whoever wants to could be a neutral country, like Switzerland. But when I glance over at Eric and Derek, they look like an army of Panzer tanks ready to do Panzer pranks, gathered on my border.

YES, SIR.

TARGET →

BYSTANDER

I LOVE A GOOD JOKE.

CHAPTER 4
PRANKENSTEIN

SEARCHING THE DEPTHS OF ONE'S MIND

← CUTAWAY VIEW

HAPPY BUG

HINGE →

This is not fun anymore. In self-defense, I'm forced back into the laboratory of fiendish pranks. Maybe if I can create the ultimate one, everybody else will leave me alone. It will be like a nuclear deterrent. But what?

DANCING

COOL AND CRAZY GUY →

Now I'm wandering down the dark halls of Prankenstein Castle, opening closed doors and peering into dark rooms. I rule out putting crazy glue on ice cream sticks and doorknobs as too cruel—even in self-defense.

Putting plastic wrap on the toilet seat is too gross. Well, I still have one solid idea—putting Mom's pantyhose into the freezer. But she would never play a trick on me, so I need to rethink the whole situation.

24

HUBIE'S THINKING CAP

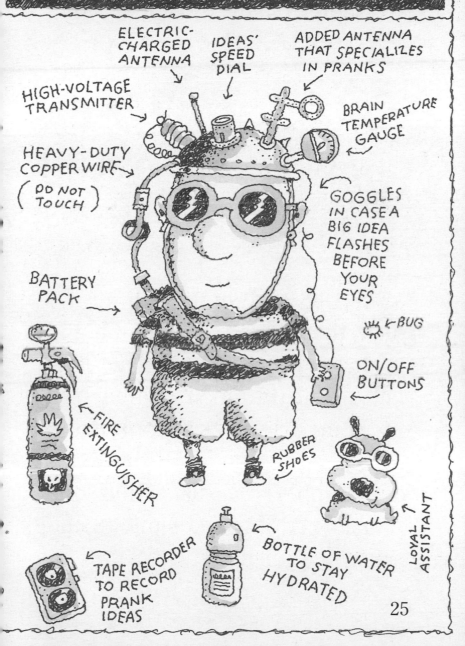

ELECTRIC-CHARGED ANTENNA

IDEAS' SPEED DIAL

ADDED ANTENNA THAT SPECIALIZES IN PRANKS

HIGH-VOLTAGE TRANSMITTER

BRAIN TEMPERATURE GAUGE

HEAVY-DUTY COPPER WIRE
(DO NOT TOUCH)

GOGGLES IN CASE A BIG IDEA FLASHES BEFORE YOUR EYES

BATTERY PACK

←BUG

ON/OFF BUTTONS

←FIRE EXTINGUISHER

RUBBER SHOES

LOYAL ASSISTANT

TAPE RECORDER TO RECORD PRANK IDEAS

BOTTLE OF WATER TO STAY HYDRATED

25

CHAPTER 5
PRANKLESS

As the end of March draws near, the tension mounts. I begin to have prankmares. The legs fall off all the chairs when I sit in them; live frogs emerge from the lasagna; and all the cups are dribble glasses. Then one morning Mom wakes me up and says, "It's April first!"

27

I dress quickly. I put on rubber boots and a raincoat, plus whatever other protective gear I can find. I load my pranks into my pockets and wait for the school bus. When it arrives, everyone is unusually calm. I put the whoopee cushion down under Penny but she just sits in another seat. I try to shake hands with Eric, using my hand buzzer, but he won't shake. This is not good— everyone is too awake.

← HAND BUZZER

HIGH PROTECTIVE GEAR

O ← MARBLE

REAR VIEW MIRRORS →

FOOTBALL HELMET ↓

← BIRD

GUM →

CATCHER'S MASK AND CHEST PROTECTOR →

→ BUG

RAINCOAT ↓

SHIELD ↗

PIZZA ↖

O TINY PLANET

THICK GLOVES ←

PADDED PANTS →

← UMBRELLA

ELEPHANT

STEEL-TOED RUBBER BOOTS

GRRR...

WATCH DOG ↑

BONE ← ⟵

O ← CIRCLE

29

CHAPTER 6
OUTPRANKED

Finally, in desperation, when we get to school I put the whoopee cushion down on Mrs. Green's chair. She comes in and sits down—*FARZZZZ!*

PICKLE BUG →

FROG WORM→

She is not happy. She holds up the limp whoopee cushion. Unfortunately, it has my name on it—caught by thc pride of ownership! She sends me and my cushion down to Miss Demeanor's office.

← HUMAN HAIR

"Well, Hubie," Miss Demeanor says. "What's this all about?"

"It's about April first," I say.

Miss Demeanor looks at her calendar. "Hubie, it's only March thirty-first," she says.

GOOD LUCK.

BEWARE →

I'M DOOMED.

I stare at the squares in disbelief. It is! It's March 31st. I've been pranked by my own mom. My own flesh and blood. How could she do this to her own innocent son? Her pantyhose are going into the freezer as soon as I get home.

← TINY HOUSE (EXACT SIZE)

← NICE PUPPY

32

BUGMAN →

CHAPTER 7
PRANKFURTERS

"Mom, how could you have done it to me?"

"April Fools." She smiles as she puts my hot dog dinner on the table.

"But, Mom—it's March."

"March Fools." She laughs.

I bite into my hot dog. Oh, no, it's rubber! Mom smiles again.

Not only have I been tricked twice already, but all the kids in school think I jumped the gun—a real sneak attack. I have broken the unwritten law—the code of the jungle. Now I'm fair game for everyone.

FAIR GAME

STAY CALM.

CHAPTER 8

P-DAY

Talk about bad dreams! I'm floating on a raft made of cheese in the middle of the ocean with seven large mice. They each have the face of one of my friends. The biggest one looks like my mom.

← SHOE   ← POLISH

I wake up with a headache. I go into the bathroom and check the toothpaste to make sure it isn't shoe polish. I check the faucet knobs to be sure the hot isn't the cold. I'm not safe anywhere.

← HAPPY CAR

"Come to breakfast," sings my mom.

Oh great, she's probably put mayonnaise in my yogurt cup. I need a food taster like the old kings used to have.

MAYONNAISE PRANK

1. SPOON OUT THE YOGURT. KEEP THE CUP.

2. FILL THE CUP WITH MAYONNAISE.

3. PLACE CUP ON KITCHEN TABLE AS USUAL.

4. SING THE VICTIM'S NAME TELLING HIM BREAKFAST IS READY.

5. YELL, "APRIL FOOLS" WHEN VICTIM IS SPITTING OUT MAYONNAISE.

6. RUN.

← CAMERA

← MAYONNAISE
CUP → ← SPOON

TABLE →

"What's the matter, Hubie? Why are you smelling the yogurt?"

"Because according to you, it's April second."

"Oh, Hubie, can't you take a little prank? And by the way, have you seen my pantyhose?"

40

CHAPTER 9
WALKING THE PRANK

Waiting for the school bus is like waiting for an ambulance. Before the day is over I may need one. The bus comes, but it doesn't stop. It passes me right by. Then T-Rex backs up.

He opens the door and shouts, "April Fools."

Oh no, him, too!

BUS DRIVER →

41

I step on and check my seat for devices. I should have brought a metal detector. It's all clear, so I sit down. All the kids start laughing. I don't know why until I try to get off the bus. My shoes are stuck to the floor. It's going to be a long day.

INSIDE OF BUS →

GLUE ↑

NEW KID →

PIMPLE ←

BAD IDEA PRANK #3
DEREK, DID YOU PUT THE PLASTIC SPIDER ON PENNY'S TRAY?
NO, MRS. BELCH, I PUT THE RUBBER SNAKE ON DORIS'S TRAY AND HAVE ALREADY BEEN PUNISHED.
ROCK

CHAPTER 10
PRANKS-A-LOT

When we get to school there's a sign on the door—SCHOOL CLOSED TODAY. We're about to go home when Mr. Bender, the principal, opens the door and shouts, "April Fools!" Boy, that was cruel.

44

PIZZA →

In class, Mrs. Green announces that we have to take the CAT test. Then she opens a box and pulls out a kitty.

"APRIL FOOLS!" She smiles. We spend the whole morning playing with the kitten, which we name April.

AHHH.

GEEE.

CUTE.

SQUEEZE → KETCHUP

In the cafeteria there's a big to-do when Eric loosens the tops of all the salt shakers and Freddy notices that someone has put hot sauce in the ketchup bottle, which sends him rushing to the bathroom. But he goes into the wrong one because someone has switched the signs.

KID FROM MARS

BOW →

WHAT'S GOING ON?

WHO WOULD DO SUCH A THING?

← HAIR

FREDDY ↓

SALT SHAKER

TOP

← SALT

ORANGE JUICE

GUM

47

Pandemonium follows, and a food fight breaks out. Tacos are flying amidst meatball missiles. Now I know what they mean by fast food. Coach Kong is about to blow his whistle but someone has filled it with water. Luckily, the recess bell rings and we all put away our trays and walk to the playground.

TACO

MEATBALL

I CAN'T BLOW MY WHISTLE.

WATER

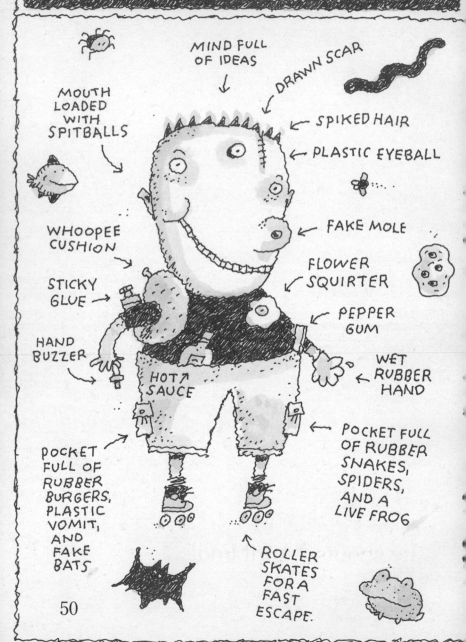

THE PRANKSTER

MIND FULL OF IDEAS

DRAWN SCAR

SPIKED HAIR

PLASTIC EYEBALL

MOUTH LOADED WITH SPITBALLS

FAKE MOLE

WHOOPEE CUSHION

FLOWER SQUIRTER

STICKY GLUE

PEPPER GUM

HAND BUZZER

HOT SAUCE

WET RUBBER HAND

POCKET FULL OF RUBBER BURGERS, PLASTIC VOMIT, AND FAKE BATS

POCKET FULL OF RUBBER SNAKES, SPIDERS, AND A LIVE FROG

ROLLER SKATES FOR A FAST ESCAPE.

50

CHAPTER 11
PRANK YOU

At recess, Derek has put super-glue on the soccer ball and it sticks to my foot. Coach Kong has moved the goals miles apart and raised the basketball hoop to 50 feet. The rest of the afternoon is pretty uneventful until Randy moves the clock hands to three o'clock. We all start packing up to go home when he shouts, "April Fools!"

Mrs. Green sees that we're all in deep shock so she takes us to the library for storytime. Mrs. Beamster reads *The Librarian from the Black Lagoon* to us.

SIT DOWN, CHILDREN.

Then she tells us it was written about her. She says she knows the author and the illustrator and that she posed for the drawings.

But then she smiles and says, "APRIL FOOLS!"

I DON'T REALLY KNOW THEM, BUT I DID SPEAK TO MIKE THALER ON AN AIRPLANE ONCE.

I'M A BIG FAN OF YOURS.

Now it *is* three o'clock and we all pile onto the school bus. Eric pretends to throw up and puts plastic vomit on Penny's seat. She screams. You can't beat the good old classics.

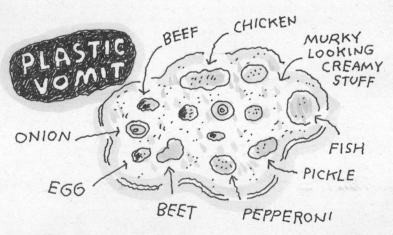

PLASTIC VOMIT

BEEF
CHICKEN
MURKY LOOKING CREAMY STUFF
ONION
FISH
EGG
BEET
PEPPERONI
PICKLE

55

MICROWAVE OVEN →

← PANTYHOSE

CHAPTER 12
PRANKS FOR THE MEMORIES

When I get home, Mom is defrosting her pantyhose in the microwave. She tells me to hurry and put on my Cub Scout uniform—there's an important meeting at four o'clock. I run to my room and change. Then I race out to the car and hop in. As I'm buckling up she starts to laugh. Oh no, not again!

FUTURE LEADER OF TOMORROW →

SIDEKICK ↓

MANY BADGES ←

SUN ↓

SPIDER ←

"Hey, Hubie." She smiles. "Since we're in the car, let's go get some ice cream. By the way, where are the car keys?"

I dig them out of my pocket and we drive to the ice-cream parlor. Mr. Cohn, the owner, says today he only has vanilla.

Vanilla's okay with something on it, but by itself it's a non-flavor, a blank piece of paper.

Then he smiles and shouts, "APRIL FOOLS!"

I get a waffle cone with a scoop of double chocolate and bubble gum pineapple ripple. All in all, it turned out to be a pretty fun day. I hear they're going to have one on the first of every month—January Fools' Day, February Fools' Day, March Fools' Day…

APRIL FOOLS' DAY!

HUBIE, YOUR MOM ASKED ME TO PLAY A PRANK ON YOU.

* HISTORICAL NOTE:
APRIL FOOLS' DAY WAS INVENTED BY BENJAMIN PRANKLIN WHEN HE ACCIDENTALLY HELD THE FIRST, AND LAST, ANNUAL PHILADELPHIA KITE-FLYING FESTIVAL ON APRIL 1ST.
(ONLY KIDDING.)
KEY
THE WIND IS PERFECT.
IT'S GOING TO STORM, BEN.
WE NEED TO LEAVE.
PHILADELPHIA

AUTHOR'S NOTE

Some pranks are funny.

But others are mean and destructive.

Be sure that if you do play a prank on April Fools' Day, it doesn't harm anyone or anyone's property. Let all your pranks be clever, creative, and kind.

DOES NOT USE A COMPUTER.

LIVES ON A CHRISTMAS TREE FARM IN OREGON

DRESSES IN YELLOW EVERY-DAY

AUTHOR, MIKE THALER

FUTURE BLACK LAGOON MANUSCRIPT

DOES NOT WEAR A WATCH

FAN MAIL